PRAISE FOR M.

A fabulous soaring thriller.

— *TAKE OVER AT MIDNIGHT,* MIDWEST
BOOK REVIEW

Meticulously researched, hard-hitting, and suspenseful.

— *PURE HEAT,* PUBLISHERS WEEKLY,
STARRED REVIEW

Expert technical details abound, as do realistic military missions with superb imagery that will have readers feeling as if they are right there in the midst and on the edges of their seats.

— *LIGHT UP THE NIGHT,* RT REVIEWS, 4
1/2 STARS

Buchman has catapulted his way to the top tier of my favorite authors.

— FRESH FICTION

Nonstop action that will keep readers on the edge of their seats.

M L. Buchman's ability to keep the reader right in the middle of the action is amazing.

The only thing you'll ask yourself is, "When does the next one come out?"

The first...of (a) stellar, long-running (military) romantic suspense series.

I knew the books would be good, but I didn't realize how good.

Buchman mixes adrenalin-spiking battles and brusque military jargon with a sensitive approach.

— PUBLISHERS WEEKLY

13 times "Top Pick of the Month"

— NIGHT OWL REVIEWS

Tom Clancy fans open to a strong female lead will clamor for more.

— *DRONE*, PUBLISHERS WEEKLY

Superb! Miranda is utterly compelling!

— *BOOKLIST,* STARRED REVIEW

Miranda Chase continues to astound and charm.

— BARB M.

Escape Rating: A. Five Stars! OMG just start with *Drone* and be prepared for a fantastic binge-read!

— READING REALITY

The best military thriller I've read in a very long time. Love the female characters.

— *DRONE,* SHELDON MCARTHUR,
FOUNDER OF THE MYSTERY
BOOKSTORE, LA

SOLO CROSSING

A SAILING ROMANCE STORY

M. L. BUCHMAN

Receive a free book and discover more by this author at: www.mlbuchman.com

Cover images:

Boat Sailing in center of storm formation © brickena

SIGN UP FOR M. L. BUCHMAN'S NEWSLETTER TODAY

and receive:
Release News
Free Short Stories
a Free Book

Get your free book today. Do it now.
free-book.mlbuchman.com

Other works by M. L. Buchman: *(* - also in audio)*

Action-Adventure Thrillers

Dead Chef
One Chef!
Two Chef!

Miranda Chase
Drone*
Thunderbolt*
Condor*
Ghostrider*
Raider*
Chinook*
Havoc*
White Top*
Start the Chase*

Science Fiction / Fantasy

Deities Anonymous
Cookbook from Hell: Reheated
Saviors 101

Single Titles
Monk's Maze
the Me and Elsie Chronicles

Contemporary Romance

Eagle Cove
Return to Eagle Cove
Recipe for Eagle Cove
Longing for Eagle Cove
Keepsake for Eagle Cove

Love Abroad
Heart of the Cotswolds: England
Path of Love: Cinque Terre, Italy

Where Dreams
Where Dreams are Born
Where Dreams Reside
Where Dreams Are of Christmas*
Where Dreams Unfold
Where Dreams Are Written
Where Dreams Continue

Non-Fiction

Strategies for Success
Managing Your Inner Artist/Writer
Estate Planning for Authors*
Character Voice
Narrate and Record Your Own
Audiobook*

Short Story Series by M. L. Buchman:

Action-Adventure Thrillers

Dead Chef

Miranda Chase Origin Stories

Romantic Suspense

Antarctic Ice Fliers

US Coast Guard

Contemporary Romance

Eagle Cove

Other

Deities Anonymous (fantasy)

Single Titles

The Emily Beale Universe
(military romantic suspense)

The Night Stalkers
MAIN FLIGHT
The Night Is Mine
I Own the Dawn
Wait Until Dark
Take Over at Midnight
Light Up the Night
Bring On the Dusk
By Break of Day
Target of the Heart
Target Lock on Love
Target of Mine
Target of One's Own
NIGHT STALKERS HOLIDAYS
*Daniel's Christmas**
*Frank's Independence Day**
*Peter's Christmas**
Christmas at Steel Beach
*Zachary's Christmas**
*Roy's Independence Day**
*Damien's Christmas**
Christmas at Peleliu Cove

Henderson's Ranch
*Nathan's Big Sky**
*Big Sky, Loyal Heart**
*Big Sky Dog Whisperer**
*Tales of Henderson's Ranch**

Shadow Force: Psi
*At the Slightest Sound**
*At the Quietest Word**
*At the Merest Glance**
*At the Clearest Sensation**

White House Protection Force
*Off the Leash**
*On Your Mark**
*In the Weeds**

Firehawks
Pure Heat
Full Blaze
*Hot Point**
*Flash of Fire**
Wild Fire
SMOKEJUMPERS
*Wildfire at Dawn**
*Wildfire at Larch Creek**
*Wildfire on the Skagit**

Delta Force
*Target Engaged**
*Heart Strike**
*Wild Justice**
*Midnight Trust**

Emily Beale Universe Short Story Series
The Night Stalkers
The Night Stalkers Stories
The Night Stalkers CSAR
The Night Stalkers Wedding Stories
The Future Night Stalkers

Delta Force
Th Delta Force Shooters
The Delta Force Warriors

Firehawks
The Firehawks Lookouts
The Firehawks Hotshots
The Firebirds

White House Protection Force
Stories

Future Night Stalkers
Stories (Science Fiction)

ABOUT THIS BOOK

When a man loses everything,
that is when the possibilities begin.

RON HAD IT ALL: THE CAREER, THE BIG HOUSE, THE SAILING
hobby, the great girlfriend. He always looked ahead,
never behind. Never had to. Until the day it all went away.

Left with nothing but his boat and a childhood dream
of circumnavigating the globe, he set sail, looking for the
future.

When a storm lashes him during his first crossing, he
finally looks at what he left behind.

1

Strain of Juan de Luca
Washington State
1/2 kilometer offshore

THE TEMPERATURE DROPPED A FEW DEGREES AS RON'S sailboat broke free of the Strait and rode out onto the broad Pacific Ocean off the Washington coast. The slight change to the sky-blue, sun-warmed May day shouldn't have sent a shiver across his shoulders, but it took an act of will to stop it.

For better or worse he'd done it, and felt as if he'd shed a hundred pounds.

That was a good sign, right?

Actually, a lot more weight than that. Someone had once told him that the tidal flow through the Strait of Juan de Fuca was four billion gallons. Every twelve hours, sixteen cubic kilometers of seawater rushed in and back out along its hundred-and-sixty-kilometer length. Around the thousand inlets and islands of Puget Sound and the inside passage of Vancouver Island, the tide rose and fell three meters twice a day. And now that massive flow had flushed his sailboat out into the Pacific Ocean like a piece of flotsam.

No, thoughtlessly aiming ahead was his past. *Climb the corporate ladder. Buy a nicer house. Drive a better car. Work waaaay too many hours.* Starting today, rather than passively riding the tides of his own life, he could make choices.

He'd dug his own burnout hole fair and square. Worse, he'd spent over a decade turning that rut into a mine-deep trench. It was only now that he was starting to see its vast, dark depths.

A rut with a view. Hell of an upgrade, Ron.

For the first time, maybe ever, he saw the cascading pile-up of his life to date. Like a whole chain of cars on a foggy interstate. And it had all been his own doing. To himself.

It was a struggle, but Ron managed not to puke over the side of the boat. Once he suppressed that urge as well, he repointed the boat to stop the flapping of the sails.

This was a new chapter...or "the last act of a desperate man." He really didn't need Sheriff Bart from *Blazing Saddles* pointing out the possibility that this was the most colossal mistake he'd ever made, which would be saying something.

The whole crowd of gulls that had been screaming overhead, asking if he was a fishing boat, ceased their constant inquiries and settled onto the waves or flew back to shore. One by one they fell behind until only the occasional bird swooped down to see if he was interesting before continuing on its way.

Nothing at all like a fishing boat, his forty-eight-foot Cheoy Lee was a sailboat designed for an ocean crossing. She was fiberglass white with mahogany trim and handrails. Clean lines, cutter rigged with a single tall mast, and he especially liked the mid-ship's cockpit tucked under the main boom. Rather than low in the stern, the ship's wheel and U-shaped teak bench seat perched a third of the way forward. He had a cloth dodger with plastic windows when he needed sun protection in the tropics, but here in the mild Pacific Northwest, he liked being open to the wind and occasional bits of spray.

Ron eyed the land to the north and south warily in case it was some kind of trick and those sixteen cubic kilometers were about to suck him back into his old life. The strait was twenty kilometers wide here, from the southern curve of Vancouver Island, a dark green line to the north, to Cape Flattery, close aboard to the south. More importantly to the Cape Flattery lighthouse on Tatoosh Island.

He'd always thought that Tatoosh looked like an upside-down saucepan half-sunk in the ocean when he'd viewed it from land. The circular island lay a kilometer offshore the northwesternmost point of the continental US. Its ten-story-tall vertical cliffs and flat top three hundred meters across was only broken by the old lighthouse and a handful of trees hardy enough to claw upward despite the horrendous storms that so often battered this section of the coast.

Open water lay to his right and Tatoosh had definitely fallen several degrees behind the port beam of the *Brise*. He was definitely at sea.

He'd wanted to name his Cheoy Lee 48 *Mu*—after H. P. Lovecraft's lost continent. Teresa had pointed out that naming a sailboat after a mythical land was one thing. But naming it after a mythical land that had sunk forever beneath the ocean after a war with Atlantis might not be the best idea.

He didn't speak French, but she did, and she'd made *Breeze* sound so lovely in that language that he'd caved easily. She'd always been able to do that to him since the first time she'd asked him out for pizza.

Ron stared upward at his sails, blinding in the sunny morning sun despite his sunglasses, and drawing well with the northwesterlies as he turned downwind. Then he looked out at the long eight-foot rollers driving landward. Last landfall for these waves had probably been the Aleutian Islands or Japan at twice the distance. Maybe even New Zealand at twice that again.

He drew in a deep breath of air so fresh it might have been newly created for his use alone. The cleansing flow almost tickled as it dragged the crap out of his lungs.

The corporate crap.

The house renovation crap that had taken up every spare moment and dollar when he wasn't scrambling to keep a computer network functional on an office-wide scale.

The whole social scene crap that he'd always sucked at, and felt incompetent about every time he was somehow snared in by his friends. At least the few friends who hadn't shed him as too much bother long ago.

He nudged the wheel over a few points and eased the sails to match the new heading. His first planned landfall would be in San Francisco for his deep-sea adventure. There were sea stacks to well off the coast, but fifty kilometers offshore would leave him plenty of leeway and still place him within ten hours of reaching port in a storm. Less if he used the engine.

The only other time he'd been out on the open ocean he'd been nine years old with Dad. The feeling of freedom had been terribly exhilarating and remarkably brief.

Every summer since before he could remember, the family had spent two weeks in a small cottage on the Cape Cod shore with other friends in nearby rentals. It was the big annual outing for the family and for their fourteen-foot Sunfish sailboat. One family had a ski boat, another a small dinghy with an outboard good for puttering out to the best mid-harbor sandbars for digging clams. The Sunfish was a sprightly sailer that Ron had mastered by the time he was seven, at least on calm waters.

One bright day, he and Dad had taken the Sunfish through the cut that separated Nauset Harbor, with plenty of good sailing for such a small boat, out onto the Atlantic.

Ron twisted to look behind him as if he could see across the continent to that long-ago adventure. *Three thousand miles and twenty years away, dude.*

They hadn't made it more than a hundred yards

offshore. A big wave had capsized them mere minutes from shore. They'd had lifejackets, and it was a common occurrence in the tiny boat and easily rectified under normal conditions. If there hadn't been a handy sandbar to duck behind, it would have been much harder to right the boat in the big rollers sweeping toward the beach.

Ron laughed, though it was a sad sound that caught hard in his throat.

Back then his father had known *everything*. He was Dad after all. In retrospect, Ron could see that the big wave that had flipped them into the ocean had probably been because his father had sailed them too close to that sandbar to begin with. The rise in the ocean bed had created the big wave and the capsize had been inevitable.

And now, in his thirties, Ron knew he was a far better sailor than Dad had ever been despite all of Dad's snide comments to the contrary.

The little Sunfish sailboat had taught Ron to dream long before that brief sea adventure. A dream of circumnavigating the globe. As a pre-teen, he'd read every book he could find at the library from Cook and Bligh to Chichester and Slocum. But he wasn't supposed to be doing this first big crossing solo.

He and Pop Sam, sailing together around the world. That had been his childhood fantasy. But Pop Sam had died the year when Ron was eight, a year before even that first adventure out onto a big ocean.

Not once had he ever thought of going with his father, and in retrospect, he could finally guess why. With Dad everything was a competition and always had been. Yet sailing, whether alone in Nauset Harbor on Cape Cod or during a blustery race on Puget Sound with a crew of eight, was the one place that Ron ever felt as if everything was easy.

Yeah, a whole lot of shit he was leaving behind. And, God damn it, he was going to leave it behind *now*.

He spun the wheel to starboard then winched in the main and jib sails as he turned to head farther offshore.

Not San Francisco. He'd already been there a few times anyway. If he was going around the world then, by God, he was going around the world. He could always visit San Francisco on the way home if he still wanted to.

New life! New course! Hoo-rah! Or did military guys say *Oo-rah?* Or... *Doesn't matter. Sail on!* Yeah, he'd use that.

New life! New course! Sail on! It was good. And change from his trench-deep rut was way past due.

He'd cross the California current as he rode it south to well offshore Baja, then pick up the high side of the northern equatorial current to the west.

As if confirming the rightness of his choice, a pair of dolphins slid in front of him, coming from somewhere dolphiny. Or porpoisy.

Then the Mock turtle said, 'No wise fish would go anywhere with a porpoise.'

Thank you Alice in Wonderland.

Though maybe he was going to sea with a sense of *dolphin.* If so, what did that mean? He really had to look up how to tell them apart.

As *Brise* forged ahead, the pair played in the bow waves, rarely jumping clear of the water, but enjoying the race.

Ron trimmed for a little more speed, not that he

could begin to match them, but it was fun to make it more interesting for them. For fifteen minutes they cruised along with him before disappearing as abruptly as they'd arrived. Did dolphins, or porpoises, have underwater teleportation? Sonar that created a large blinking, *Fun over there!* sign in their heads? That would be cool.

Brise journeyed on without dolphins or sea gulls to keep her company. She rode well over the waves. The Cheoy Lee was a perfect compromise between a lean uncomfortable racing boat and a slow, fat and wallowing cruiser. Big enough to be comfortable as a liveaboard and narrow enough to move well. The only sounds were the slight slap of the rigging as he crested each wave, the continuous background rush of water peeled open by his fin keel, and the shushing of the ocean closing behind him, leaving no more than a whitish patch of water, full of turbulated air that dissipated quickly.

With all the lines routed into the cockpit, she was easy to single-hand. No crew required, just he and *Brise.* It was enough.

Next stop Hawaii. His wide swing to the south, rather than striking for the most direct line across the easter gyre of the North Pacific, should provide much steadier winds.

Maybe he'd find a worthy sailing companion there.

It certainly hadn't been Teresa Compton.

2
_____

Heceta Bank
Oregon Coast
87 km offshore

RON STUFFED IN HIS EARPLUGS AND YANKED UP HIS HOOD before clawing his way up onto deck. The moment he opened the hatch, the rain drummed against his rain slicks.

It had been maddeningly loud until he'd located where he'd stowed the earplugs—squished up bits of toilet paper hadn't cut it. At least it was a cool rain so that he wouldn't sweat to death under the slicks. He did end up being clammy all day, with cold little rivulets finding the odd gap to soak his clothes in scattered, annoying ways.

Up on deck, he snapped his safety harness onto the jack line first and closed the hatch behind him second. The line ran bow-to-stern along the deck. If he fell, the short line would keep him aboard the boat, or at least attached to it.

It wasn't really called for in this weather as the seas weren't particularly rough—as if the rain was beating it flat. But he was already staggeringly tired and he didn't trust himself not to stumble overboard. The boat was heeled fifteen degrees and the lifelines that ran around the entire perimeter of the deck were only thigh high. He couldn't escape the image of sliding down the deck and having the lifeline toss him in a head-over-heels somersault into the waves rushing by so close.

Brise's autopilot would keep heading the boat south-southwest leaving him behind to drown on his own.

To sleep. Perchance to dream. Hamlet, buddy, you had it easy. At least you were on dry land.

The Cheoy Lee handled well but he was not adapted to sleeping while rolling side-to-side as they climbed and descended the rollers at an angle. And with each roll, every line slapped or twanged or twinged or found another new sound to make. Slapping sounds were the domain of the waves against the fiberglass hull. With each crested wave, the mast swung left then right, then left again, snapping the sail loudly as it refilled to draw ahead.

He also hadn't slept well because of general paranoia. He knew that would ease with time, but last night he'd stuck his head up through the hatch every thirty minutes, sometimes every twenty, to inspect that everything was as it should be. He was running across the massively busy shipping lanes of the US West Coast and it was all too easy to imagine being run down.

Ron blinked up into the rain as he settled by the wheel in the cockpit. It was hard to believe that the little foot-across ball of the aluminum radar reflector near the mast top was brighter on a ship's radar than the rest of his boat combined. Wet cloth sails returned notoriously little signal and the rounded aluminum mast scattered rather than reflected any radar sweep from another ship.

That was assuming that any approaching ship had a crew that was actually paying attention.

There was a horror story common enough for him to believe it had happened. It was of a ship coming into port, only to have a dockhand point in surprise at the mast and sails snagged on the anchor with no sailboat attached. Even when he'd managed to wedge himself where the berth's mattress met the hull to stop his rolling about, that fear—but one of many—had kept him awake.

The guard zone setting on Ron's marine radar should do the job of waking him if there were problems, like an approaching ship. But experience hadn't yet built trust in that either. Sure, it had worked fine in Puget Sound, but what about out here on the ocean. His brain knew it was fine, but his nervous system was twitchier than a rebooting server with configuration issues. Maybe, if he mounted a second small wind turbine in the rigging to doubly ensure that the batteries stayed charged to run the equipment, his nerves would chill. Probably not.

On deck and conscious not by choice, he did his morning routine.

Only Day Three since driving past Tatoosh Island and already he had a routine. That had to be another good sign.

Embrace routine. Because you're sure too tired to actually think. A good maxim that he should write down somewhere...somewhere that wasn't soaked to the skin by the unending rain drilling against his slicks and pounding on the deck. *A bright cheerful patter on a tin roof? Not!*

He walked up the length of the deck, checking each line and fitting as he went. The jack line had been run down the port side, so he trailed his harness clip along behind him which banged and clattered over every fitting and winch. He was too unstable on his feet to keep it lifted off the deck.

For the return, he hadn't rigged a line down the starboard side. Ducking back and forth under the sails, around the dinghy tied upside down to the deck, and offering a brief prayer to the white canister of the life raft that he'd never need it, had been arduous enough the first two days. But he didn't have the energy to rig a second jack line today as he'd meant to yesterday.

"Fine. It all looks good from here." His voice was the first sound he'd heard not made by the boat or the ocean since he'd left behind the gulls off the Strait of Juan de Fuca.

He sounded like a dying frog.

"You're all alone. It's okay to talk to yourself." Not much better. And was that true? Or was he losing it?

He liked music, but he'd been told so often that he sang flat that he'd given up singing along to anything, even in the car. The thought of going below to plug in something on the stereo had him staring aloft at the wind generator again. Six little blades in a three-foot housing

—it was *supposed* to produce plenty of power. But he needed the energy for nav and radio gear. He didn't *need* the music.

Ron stayed on deck.

"So where are we?" As if he didn't already know. Nope! The sound of his voice was too sad all alone on the ocean. Maybe he'd keep his thoughts to himself just as *Brise* kept her thoughts to herself.

He looked east. The sheeting rain limited visibility to perhaps a kilometer. Sitting once more in the cockpit, the horizon was only five kilometers anyway. And the nearest land was a hundred.

Even though he'd sprung for the unit that could read down to seven hundred meters, the depth sounder said the bottom was beyond range. He shut it off to save power.

Brise was out over the great deep and the abyssal plain lay three kilometers below. Even the great Heceta Bank section of the continental shelf lay well to the east of him.

And beyond the Heceta Bank lay Heceta Head and the Heceta Lighthouse Bed and Breakfast.

It had been his and Teresa's first vacation together. They'd been dating for six months and she'd wanted to drive down the Oregon Coast. A fan of her mystery novels had gifted her a night in the B&B, which was their southernmost stop. They'd wandered down the coast for three days, following Highway 101's lazy meanderings through quaint towns and tacky tourist enclaves that still smelled of the sea and endured the battering of the raw Pacific Ocean.

They'd strolled through the surprisingly interesting

Columbia River Maritime Museum, eaten fish and chips at Mo's in Lincoln City like any good tourist, and been skunked on a whale sightseeing day out of the "World's Smallest Harbor" in Depoe Bay. It had been such a lovely day that they hadn't cared about the lack of whales. Their relationship had still been in that early phase where they couldn't be in close enough contact.

Together they'd gazed out at the deep ocean to where he sailed even now. That's when he'd told her of his silly childhood dream of sailing around the world with his grandfather. Teresa had done as she always did whenever he had an idea: *You should do it!*

As if it was so easy.

He'd been starting a new corporate job the day they returned from their drive. A promotion to head a key department after a series of unrelated turnovers had coincided to gut the group. They'd tasked him with keeping it afloat and improving the overall operation while he was at it. It was the biggest project he'd ever tackled and the first time he'd done one for a national-level corporation. There was room to climb here in ways that none of his past positions at smaller firms had offered.

She'd kept after him for the rest of the trip. In her gentle way, of course: cheerful, easy-going...and tenacious as hell.

So what would be your first port of call?

When they'd stopped at Newport's harbor, she'd insisted that they stroll along the waterfront.

Could any of these boats in the marina cross the ocean?

He had done a fair amount of sailing, moments

stolen from work over the years. Occasionally running in races up and down Puget Sound. He'd risen to the point that it wasn't unusual for a skipper to call him in to helm the boat for a race that the skipper himself couldn't attend. His favorite had been a Swan 60 cruiser/racer that had handled like a dream. They weren't major races, first prize was often little more than bragging rights, and he'd earned that several times.

Teresa had even hauled him into a brokerage. She knew nothing about boats. They'd spent hours, with her charming both himself and broker, touring the different types of boats as an *education for her.*

She had made it seem like a game, a bit of whimsical fun to enliven their trip. But the idea had begun to take form in the back of his mind as perhaps more than a childhood dream. Somehow he'd never connected the idea of getting on a boat whenever he could break away from work, with that long-lost idea.

At Heceta Head, they'd toured the old lighthouse and relaxed to watch the sunset from the wide front porch of the keeper's cottage turned B&B. The air had smelled as fresh there as it ever had in his life. Teresa curled up beside him under a throw blanket in an Adirondack chair meant for one. The dream seemed impossibly possible there.

Ron had known it wouldn't happen, but it wasn't a bad dream.

They'd made love in a small room facing the ocean and lit by the moonlight. A thin fog had slid in toward midnight. That, in turn, had revealed the lighthouse beam sweeping toward the great unknown, beckoning them to watch it through the night.

The gourmet seven-course breakfast, one of the B&B's trademarks, had completed the perfect night.

Teresa had grabbed a brochure of the Oregon lighthouses from the front table. They'd planned to drive back to Seattle up through the Willamette Valley, maybe even visit the wine country though neither of them knew much about it. Instead they'd returned up the coast visiting every lighthouse and scenic overlook that they'd missed on the way south.

All that seemed impossibly far away—lost in the foggy past of a year ago.

The unending drum of rain is your life now.

It already felt as if it would never end, drumming on his slicks. The fat, wind-driven drops hit hard enough to sting through the thick rubberized whatever this was. And still he was nodding in and out of a doze on the cockpit seat.

Had they been in love then?

Ron tried to remember when the *love* part of their relationship had begun but couldn't pin it down. It had been real. He remembered that much.

He strongly suspected that it had started somewhere between when she had begun to dream his dream for him, and when he'd finally begun to dream it for himself.

3

San Francisco Bay
California
169 km due west

S*TUPID   CLICHES   AND   STEREOTYPES!* T*HEY'D   ALWAYS*
bugged Ron.

But California was being true to both.

The Pineapple Express, the warm winds driving from
Hawaii toward the Oregon and Washington Coast—and
dumping eighty-three kajillion gallons of water on his
head in seven straight days—had ceased sometime in the
night. He'd drawn even with San Francisco, and Mother
Nature had shut off the faucet with one sharp twist of her
almighty hand.

Seven days, which should have taken him five, spent
battering into a head wind that had forced him to either
tack much farther offshore than he wanted to go, or sent
him racing toward land he didn't want to reach. But the
due-south course he wanted had put him in a very

uncomfortable broadside to the Express' waves. Instead he'd done the exhausting work of tacking back and forth to take the waves on one quarter or the other.

But as he sailed opposite central California, the rain had disappeared. The winds had curled in behind him until they were smooth northerlies. The silence as he spread the sails to dead downwind was almost haunting —no whistling wind in the rigging, no pounding rain, no hard slap of wave or sail.

Brise rushed effortlessly ahead.

He now cruised at nearly the same speed as the low rollers. Rather than being slammed every ten or fifteen seconds, the long swells caught up with him every few minutes, gently lifting the stern of the *Brise,* sweeping smoothly underneath, and then setting the bow down like a giant rocking chair.

And, to complete the cliché, the sun now glittered off the bluest rolling ocean. The last of the storm clouds lingered far to the north as no more than a low fog soon forgotten. The more distance the better.

For twelve hundred kilometers, he'd managed not to turn back. Not to give in to the urge to turn for port, sell the damned boat, and fly home.

But then he'd be yet another person who had dared to dream—and failed.

"I tried, but it was too much bother." The perfect sunny day scoffed at him when he tried out different versions aloud. "It was so much harder than I expected." No one had promised him it would be easy.

Nothing had been easy in his life. Except maybe Teresa. Maybe that had been the final problem.

He remembered talking with his boss at a law firm where Ron had run the IT for a major case, tracking and coding five million pages of project documents spread across five states and three continents. Fred had all the trappings of success: a founder and named partner of one of Seattle's Top Ten law firms, the fancy house, still married to his college girlfriend, kids all successfully launched, and he was about to retire to luxury.

Got out of school and decided that life sucked. So, I did what I was supposed to do but can't say as I ever enjoyed it much.

When Ron had mentioned the conversation to Dad, he'd shrugged a maybe. Just what Ron had always wanted to be, a key player in his father's disappointing life. He certainly wasn't going to do that with his own.

Sure he was a nerd and a geek. But unlike his engineer father who was only good with machines, Ron had struggled for more. He'd learned how to be good with people, or at least better than the average computer nerd. It had made him a project manager with a tech twist. He'd escaped the programmer trap of being an asocial cog in someone else's project.

The problem had been that all of the learning and growth, all that internal work, had made it so that he didn't fit in at either end of the spectrum: the extrovert power players or the asocial geeks. Instead he'd discovered a no-man's land in between.

Shake it off! The past was clinging like barnacles on the hull and that would never do.

Action! Do something! Move about! More good maxims.

He began the cleanup of the boat that he'd avoided

during the seven days of battering rain. There was a squeak in the boom vang's upper pulley that sang with every tiny shift of the mainsail. On a frayed end on a backstay adjuster line, he snipped off the end and pulled out his splicing tools to create a clean butt end that wouldn't unravel again. He made the rounds with a big screwdriver to make sure that all of the tracks were well snugged down.

Without really being conscious he was doing it, he had begun looking for a sailboat six months after that trip to Heceta Head with Teresa.

He'd asked a skipper of a Valiant 40 if he wanted a hand for a Saturday sail so that he could see how that particular boat handled.

An old guy ran an older fifty-six-foot wooden bugeye ketch as a dinner-cruise sailboat. He'd treated Teresa to an evening sail but spent most of his time chatting with the skipper about cruising. Tony had spent years crossing from Puget Sound in the summer to Corpus Christi, Texas in the winters. Twice each year through the Panama Canal—singlehanded.

Ron had started focusing on sailing solo after that. Sometimes he'd borrow a boat. Other times, he'd go out with a like-minded sailor, but with only one of them managing the whole boat at a time.

Sail *with* someone?

Since the dream of sailing with Pop Sam had died with his grandfather, he'd always sort of assumed he'd sail alone.

But now Teresa was in his life. Would she want to go offshore with him? He almost asked her a hundred different times, but always found a reason not to. When they celebrated their one-year dating anniversary, it had been the longest he'd ever been with anyone. He didn't want to mess that up.

Six months after that…

Yeah. Six months after that, the real opportunity had come up. Everything had seemed to happen at once.

So damned fast. He looked up at the sky. *Universe, were you kicking my butt?* It was something Teresa often talked about.

When everything is moving a little to fast, you're in the flow of right action.

Like the universe knows more about what's good for me than I do? he'd asked.

She nodded an *of course* in that way of hers.

What had happened was a buddy on the sailor circuit knew someone selling a Cheoy Lee 48. Designed by Bob Perry in 1980 as an offshore racing/cruiser. The owner had run it in the Vic-Maui race a few times, but wanted a smaller boat, a daysailer to bob about on Lake Washington now that he had a family.

Teresa had been deep in drafting a fresh murder plot for her next book. When she was like that, she couldn't be distracted by anything, except Chinese takeout. In the end run of a novel, even that didn't do it. He'd learned that he was on his own at such times.

She'd sailed with him as often as not and had quickly learned to be a capable deckhand. But while going offshore wasn't her passion, it had slowly become his.

He'd taken the Cheoy Lee 48 out once with the owner and knew he'd found his boat. As soon as the marine surveyor had signed off on its soundness, he'd written the check. It would mean selling his house and moving aboard. Funny. He hadn't even thought about that until the deal was done.

Once he had? A space that fit him instead of the bigger-house-is-better image he'd inherited from Dad. He sold the house fully furnished. No yard maintenance! *Oh yeah!* House maintenance traded for boat maintenance? *Any damn day of the week.*

Ron knelt on the deck and scrubbed cleanser across the fiberglass decking. The clip on his safety harness had left marks on the white surface as he'd dragged it up and down the jack line for the entire last week.

The autopilot was holding him steady on the wind.

He no longer had to remember to look up for passing ships that might cause him trouble. Every minute or so, he did a quick scan around automatically, barely noticing the break in his rhythm.

Proactive. Efficiency. He was rocking this new life.

San Francisco was one of the busiest ports on the West Coast and the clutter of sea traffic reflected that. But the Seattle / Tacoma Port Alliance was bigger and in much more confined waters. Out here on the open ocean, the clutter of ships was actually spread quite far apart.

Also, the radar had beeped its alarm enough times now for him to trust its judgement.

Early on, Ron had second-guessed the impulse purchase of *Brise* a thousand times. But now that he was sailing smoothly beneath the shining Californian sunshine, he could feel that weight sloughing off as well.

By the time Teresa had emerged from her writing,

he'd already moved what he was keeping onto the boat and had his house up for sale. He'd showed *Brise* to her without explaining that he'd bought it already.

The moment she figured that out, she'd thrown her arms around him and wept. Not little happy tears, but great heaving sobs that had alarmed other liveaboards along the dock. Heads had popped out of hatches to make sure everything was okay, but he hadn't known how to tell.

Clueless as usual! He'd held her, unsure what else to do.

I was so afraid you'd let your dream die, she'd finally managed. *That would have been so tragic. I'd thought I'd lost you to your job.*

But he still had his job—or had at that time.

And like the idiot he was, he'd looked from her tear-stained face to the boat and back to her.

His dream?

It had merely been the next thing he'd wanted to do. He'd never quite connected it to his dream possibly coming true. The idea that he might actually chuck it all and go sailing around the world had been...surprising.

Surprising and unlikely as hell! That's what he'd though in that moment as she clung to him at the dockside.

But against all odds and doubts, it *had* come true.

He was living the dream now, wasn't he? How weird was that?

He made himself a tuna sandwich from the last of his bread, fished a couple of carrots and a can of Coke out of the refrigerator, and took it up to the cockpit. It was his first meal, more involved than an energy bar, that he'd eaten on deck since he'd left Port Townsend.

Ron leaned back in the sun. He checked the horizon, his heading, and the set of the sails in a single glance.

It was just him and *Brise* but they were on their way.

Alone.

The tuna sandwich tasted like cardboard.

4

Central Baja California
Mexico
1,193 km due west

THE SUN LASTED FOR FOUR GLORIOUS DAYS...

Then the storm caught up with the *Brise*. It was noon but it looked like the middle of the night.

Ron had seen it coming in several ways.

He'd spotted the first of it as high cirrus clouds, horse tails, off northern Baja.

The weather in Seattle had been very predictable because almost all of it came in off the Pacific without being stirred around by passing over whole sections of the continent. The high wisps typically preceded a still-high gray haze that let through most of the sunlight but blocked the blue sky. Depending on how fast the transition was, it could then be anywhere from one to three days for the heavy overcast and rain to move in.

This was coming from a different direction, but he

wondered if it would follow the same pattern. He didn't have to wonder for long.

He was off central Baja by the time the NOAA Weatherfax forecast over his long-range radio had looked worrisome. An early-season storm had been born over the heated waters of the Sea of Cortez, trapped between Baja and mainland Mexico. It had escaped into the Pacific and built rapidly over the warming north equatorial current he'd been hoping to ride west to Hawaii.

The weather radar began painting disconcerting bands of green, then yellow, and finally red.

The storm was between him and the land, so he couldn't turn east to make a run for a port, any port. Besides, with his distance offshore, it would be a three-day run, probably four or five against the prevailing winds. Any hopes of driving clear to the north or south were dashed by the storm's rapid growth. It soon spanned six hundred kilometers and he was near enough the center that he wasn't getting out of its way.

Then NOAA predicted that somewhere past his position it would shift from whole gale to the first hurricane of the season on its way to beat on Hawaii. For now it was only a Force 10 storm—only. The same strength that had devastated the Fastnet race around the UK four decades before. He'd read Rousmaniere's book, *Fastnet, Force 10*. Fifteen died, dozens of boats were abandoned, and several sank. Over a hundred were rescued by lifeboat services and helicopters.

Panic doesn't solve shit! He'd learned that when dealing with a crashed computer network or a boss who'd tipped off the deep end of rage about something.

But damn! Panic sure felt tempting, didn't it?

The biggest storm he'd ever sailed in had been thirty-five knots, forty miles an hour, in the San Juan Islands of Puget Sound. He'd watched twenty-five-foot boats getting slapped about by the story-tall waves. Luckily, he'd been aboard a fifty-foot full-keel ketch that day and she'd ridden such weather easily.

In a Force 10 storm out here on the Pacific, he'd be facing fifty-to-sixty knot winds and seas that were—he looked at the storm force table in two different references before he could quite believe it—ten- to fifteen-meter waves. He tried to imagine waves three to five stories tall and all it did was make his head hurt. The very top of his mast was only six stories tall.

Way too real!

Ignore that shit!

Go! Go! Go! Like one of those SWAT team moments in a movie. *SWAT team of one. Here I come!*

First, Ron made sure everything was well stowed and that the hatches were all battened down. He prepared two days of meals that he could simply grab and eat cold if necessary. Cooking on his small propane stove would be out of the question despite the gimble that would let it swing to stay level as the boat rocked side-to-side. If he encountered end-to-end pitching, it definitely wouldn't work.

He'd only had to reef a sail a few times in his life, so he did it well before the heavy winds hit. He lowered the main a third of the way, then went down the sail running a tie that went through each of the grommets in the middle of the sail and cinching it around the main boom.

The remaining one-third of his main looked ridiculous in the fine sailing wind he presently had, but he'd rather lose sailing time and be ready.

He left the big genoa sail drawing at the headstay that went from the tip of the bow to the top of the mast. It had roller furling, so he wouldn't even need to leave the cockpit later to roll it up around that front wire. Then he could pull out the storm jib from the fore stay that started several feet aft of the bow and attached two-thirds of the way up the mast. It was a much smaller sail so he could still have enough way on, enough speed to control the boat even in a high wind.

Hopefully.

Just in case, he spent a while studying the storm anchor. It didn't sound scary, it sounded terrifying. If the storm grew to be too awful, but before it became *too* awful, he'd have to douse sails and set the sea anchor. It was an underwater parachute twelve feet in diameter and eighteen feet long. It would drag in the sea at the end of five hundred feet of line, literally an anchor in the water. The wind and waves would drag *Brise* downwind against that line and hold her bow on into the maelstrom.

What else? What else?

Prep the crew? Just me. Done!

Set the frequency to call a May Day if everything went all Fastnet, Force 10 on him. Already done. Right. Standard practice: to always be set to the emergency frequency so that he could hear others in trouble. Done!

Crap!

Out of ideas, there was nothing to do now but worry and wait.

Six hours later, the leading edge was on him. It hadn't eased in, it had slammed. The sea rose before a wind that no longer washed over *Brise.* Instead it made the rigging hum, and then begin to whistle as it lashed the building waves ever higher.

Act early! Right!

Ron hauled the main boom tightly amidships and rolled up the storm jib. The double-reefed main sail, and hadn't putting in the second reef been a huge pain to do, kept him roughly pointed into the wind.

He fought his way out of the marginal safety of the cockpit. On hands and knees he crawled forward, with the jack line hooked to his safety harness as a guide.

Each wave slammed in from a different direction. He should have...what? Had another person on board?

Duh!

A wave, strangely warm here near the equator after years sailing in the frigid waters of Puget Sound, slammed him into the low side of the cabin. Its retreat tried to drag him through the lifelines. The next washed him aft along the deck. He could feel the heat from clutching the jack line that would have been rope burn if he hadn't pulled on fingerless bicycle gloves.

Good decision.

When he could breathe again, Ron was amazed that his autoinflate life vest hadn't decided he was underwater and triggered.

He finished the crawl forward to double-check that the line for the sea anchor was secure before he deployed it over the side. Just as he decided it was, the bow drove deep into a wave, green water slamming aboard and driving the bow even deeper into the water. He managed a half breath, thick with salt spray, and held it as he was submerged.

This time his life jacket decided he was in trouble and inflated with a hard snap against his chest.

The float pushed him to the surface at the same moment that the wave drained overboard. Instead of slamming down onto the deck, the life preserver cushioned the impact.

That's something at least.

Coughing and half gagging for breath, Ron rode the next wave back along the deck. He was almost washed past the cockpit and dumped into the stern lifelines before he could stop himself. He flopped into the cockpit and lay on one of the benches like a beached fish, until the next wave came at him sideways, high enough to reach the cockpit as he rode broadside into it.

Struggling to sit up, he tossed over the trip line so that he could recover the sea anchor later, then the sea anchor itself. He briefly snubbed the line. With a sharp jerk, the pressure on the line increased a hundred-fold and he let it run. The brief snub of the line had fully deployed the sea anchor, hopefully, and it was now an underwater parachute instead of a useless snarl of cloth.

Less than a minute later, a low thrum sounded through the boat, a deep vibration he could feel through his butt on the cockpit seat despite the pounding of the storm. The sea anchor had reached the end of its heavy rode, made of five hundred feet of three-quarter-inch nylon line and thirty feet of chain.

The bow swung into the wind and waves, and the

boat settled down almost immediately. With a couple of bungie cords he lashed the steering wheel to center the rudder, decided that *Brise* was riding well with the double-reefed main, and collapsed once more onto the cockpit's bench seat.

Did it. Without dying! Whoot!

The storm continued to howl. The wind-lashed salt spray was warm against his face as it tugged against his inflated life vest. He'd have to deal with that before he crawled forward in half an hour to make sure the sea anchor's line wasn't chafing. For now, he wasn't moving an inch.

Thousands of sailors had ridden out hundreds of storms safely enough. He could do that. The motion wasn't smooth in the storm, but he could feel the solid hold of the sea anchor keeping him safe.

Stay calm. Stay focused. Those were the keys.

Slowly he turned his attention to the world around him. The sun hadn't shown its face at all today, but now evening was settling in beyond the storm. Other than the displays for the radar and the radio he had on in the cockpit, the world would soon be pitch dark.

Was that a good thing? It would hide the waves that seemed to tower in every direction when he was in a trough, or go on forever as he crested the next. It was all beyond his control now. His life was in the hands of *Brise* and her sea anchor.

And if that wasn't enough? Lost at sea—who would know? At least that would be a familiar feeling.

Never good enough to make any impression on his narcissistic father.

The career that had blown up in his face...

He shut his eyes as he crested one last wave to shut out the vision. Even knowing that it might be too dark to see at all by the time he crested the next wave thirty seconds from now, he couldn't make himself look at his last glimpse of daylight.

He'd killed himself for John in his last job.

For twelve months, since the day after that trip with Teresa down the coast, he'd given John's firm his all. Each aspect of his job was a full-time proposition, yet together they were far more than that. John should have hired three people, maybe four, not counting the rest of the staff. But that hadn't stopped Ron from throwing himself body and soul to try and do it all.

Hero of the corporate save! Yeah, sure. How many times did you sell yourself that one, Ron?

The department he'd inherited with only a single remaining, benighted staffer had been a mission-critical step of the overall operation. It had taken four new staff and twenty-hour days not to miss their delivery deadlines. On top of that, their original operational flow would have pleased a Rube Goldberg fan. If there was a more awkward way to do each step of the necessary operations, Ron had no idea what they might be. Like they'd painted over the barnacles on a hull year after year rather than scraping it clean first. It had dragged like an old scow.

But before he could straighten *that* out, he had to fix the main problem. The core, hundred-thousand-dollar software package that made their department run, hadn't been upgraded in so long that the manufacturer neither supported nor offered training in it anymore.

Twelve months.

Ron rode the darkness down another wave face with only the dim glow of the boat's instruments casting any light. As planned he was barely making any way, held in place by his parachute anchor beneath the waves. The little half-knot of speed that he was making was going backwards, which didn't show on the meter. The compass said he was pointed east, into the waves and wind. But the storm was dragging him west, slowly, but at least toward his destination.

Unlike that damn job, though you were so sure it was, weren't you, you naive idiot?

Twelve months he'd given everything to that job, except for the rare occasions when he'd emerged to sail or outfit *Brise* right near the end he hadn't known was imminent.

And Teresa. Though nowhere near enough time spent with her.

He'd taken her on a few shakedown sails, mostly short afternoon trips. But one time he'd taken two whole days off and run from Seattle up to Orcas Island. They'd eaten at the luxurious Rosario Resort, dining on Alaskan Snow Crab Pasta and Pan-Roasted Salmon with mushroom risotto—along with an eye-searing bill. But it had been a great date...before he'd had to spend half of the return sail burning up cell time to dig out a rush project, leaving the sailing to Teresa.

He'd barely seen her since except for stolen minutes.

Then the hammer had fallen.

John had strolled up to Ron's desk on a Tuesday afternoon, an hour before Ron's presentation to a major client that he'd had little to do with previously. They were unhappy and it had been decided that Ron was the one to talk them down.

John had veered him into HR and told him to sit down.

The HR person had been halfway through her spiel before Ron had figured out what was going on.

I'm being fired? Why?

Failure to achieve defined goals. She didn't know the details but it became clear that it was the failure to upgrade that core piece of software. Sure, all he'd needed was two weeks' help from the IT guys that John would never free up—followed by a week of quiet for dedicated training of the staff on the new product that was never going to happen.

That, of course, would be stated to any possible future employer calling for a reference. And the Seattle IT project management world wasn't a big community. Once word was out, he'd be a pariah. He hadn't been fired; he'd been blacklisted.

Such complete and total bullshit! Which didn't make it any less real.

Out of other ideas, he'd sold his car, canceled his slip rental at the marina—and set sail.

Real fucking brilliant, Ron!

Now thousands of kilometers away in the middle of the storm, the anger boiled so hot that he finally couldn't keep it down. He managed to lean over the cockpit coaming and heave up the burning bile onto the outer deck. The spray would wash it out the scuppers, if he could ever stop heaving it up.

And his big dream. He was out here in the middle of the fucking ocean, in the middle of his big dream, and it was that utter bastard John who'd set him on it. Not coherent thoughts or plans. Not hope or joy.

Ron went from wet heaves, to searing bile, and finally to dry heaves.

Christ! How far past all reason had he pushed himself? He sprawled with his elbows hooked over the coaming rail. That was all that kept him from sliding into the cockpit's footwell amid the sloshing seawater.

I get it! Alright already! I get it.

Why had it taken him so long? In retrospect, he could see that the betrayal had been a long time coming. He'd never asked why the department lead and the three others had all decided to find new jobs at roughly the same time. Probably wouldn't have been told the truth if he had.

He could even see that John had decided that rather than giving the upset client a presentation—that had caused Ron three sleepless nights to build because there simply wasn't any other time to do it—why not simply fire a department head for them?

John had found an excuse, put Ron's head on a platter, and then had probably served up Ron's presentation as his own.

"Bastard!" His throat tore as he laughed and quickly fell to crying.

Tomorrow, if the storm didn't find some way to kill him first, he'd start over. He'd begin his journey at

37

some random point a thousand kilometers from anywhere.

For now? Rubbing at his eyes simply made them sting with excess salt water.

He was such a fucking mess. No wonder Teresa hadn't come to see him off when he said he was leaving.

5

Crossing out of the storm toward Hawaii

FOR THE THREE DAYS OF THE STORM RON HADN'T BEEN ABLE to keep down anything more solid than a fruit drink. It wasn't seasickness. His gut was simply wound in such a hard knot that it couldn't take in anything new.

The sea anchor, resisting the storm, had kept his drift in check. In those three days *Brise* had covered the same distance she would normally sail in eight hours.

Made it through. Safe past the storm.

After an hour spent fighting the sea anchor back aboard, he'd collapsed in simple exhaustion. For six hours straight the boat bobbed and weaved on the confused seas left behind by the storm, while he slept as if he *had* died in the storm.

This time he *did* wake up on the floor of cockpit where the motion of an unruly wave had tossed him.

Getting underway again, he began the four-thousand-kilometer haul on to Hawaii as the sky cleared and the seas settled. His course now lay well south of most shipping lanes. All the big boats had the power and urgency to ignore the best currents and winds as they simply powered along the shortest-distance great circle routes from Asia to America and back. Out here between Mexico and Hawaii, there were few intruders besides the recreational sailors.

He'd slept twenty of the next twenty-four hours and came out of it feeling half human and utterly famished.

He'd weathered his first major storm at sea, a big one. On his own. It had been utterly terrifying at times, but also good. Well...survivable.

Sure, I can solo around the world. I'm good enough. No prob!

Talk about a fall from smugness. Brutal fucking storm.

He'd survived it as he would survive the collapse of his career. This was good. Maybe a fresh start was what he needed. Time away to...do...something.

For the next ten days he had plenty to keep him busy. Drying out and repacking the sea anchor. Two of the rigging lines had taken bad chafing during the storm. As he replaced them, he was able to figure out why. One he was able to fix himself, the other one he'd need to hit a marine supply store in Hawaii so that it wouldn't happen again.

He'd thought his life's possessions had been well stowed below. Half had been. Half had ended up flung about the cabin. As he'd waded through the mess to sort it out, he wondered why he'd thought most of it was so important.

Embrace the new *life! Alice fell down the rabbit hole into Wonderland. Well, he'd climb back out before he got lost again.*

He began a give-away pile on the settee.

The table stood in the middle of the cabin, less than a foot wide with both leaves folded down. Raised, it reached the curved settee for four to sit at one side and the straight bench for three to sit on the other. He'd spent most nights on the latter, a single-wide berth he could pitch into still fully clothed not three steps from the base of the ladder to the cockpit.

He still had yet to sleep in the double-wide v-berth up in the very bow of the boat. Those extra steps had seemed too far away from the pilot's station of instruments or the cockpit ladder. And that big forward bed had been the last place he and Teresa had made love before the final apocalypse at work that had cast him so adrift.

Soon the settee was covered with junk to give away. Like more saucepans than his three-burner stove had burners, and old science fiction books that he had on his e-reader anyway.

For the throw-away pile, he expanded onto the bench seat. Patch cables and adapters for computers he no longer even owned—a few so old that *no one* still owned them. A PS/2 cable had been ridiculous twenty years ago, and he couldn't even remember the last time he'd seen a DB25 serial cable. But what a DB37 was for he couldn't remember at all. Yet he had them aboard.

Stupid talismans of a past he'd clung onto for far to long. Done with that!

He unearthed a number of things, good, expensive things, that he'd bought a second time, forgetting he'd already bought them once. Maybe he could sell those. Not for much probably.

Then the boat took a wave hard and dumped everything onto the cabin floor and mixed it all up again. After going on deck to make sure everything was okay, he sorted the...*let's be honest*...jetsam into bags that he left on the cabin floor this time.

Finally, after sorting through everything in the various deck lockers, and the galley, master bedroom, and main cabin below, there was only one area left.

The Cheoy Lee 48's center-cockpit design had one more advantage beyond its place at the center of the boat. Having the cockpit shifted a third of the way forward had a significant impact on the interior layout. The galley and main cabin were less luxurious. The navigator's station, typically a comfortable sitting area to work radios, keep a log, and even an additional pilot's berth, was now a cramped seat.

The trade-off was the addition of a rear cabin.

He knew he should go back and sort through what was in there, but he kept finding other chores to avoid that. When he caught himself trying to understand a book on marlinspike rope work so that he could make a swim ladder from scratch, he knew he was being foolish.

For the first time since he'd left port, Ron made himself follow the narrow passage that ran aft from the galley along the port side. Once past the structure of the cockpit up above, it opened into a suite far more private than the forward v-berth off the main cabin. A big bed filled part of the space. It had numerous skylights and its own hatch to flood it with sunlight. Tucked neatly around the edges of the cockpit's shape above was a second bath, complete with head, sink, and shower. There was also a small desk.

Prior to his departure, it had been crammed with gear: spare sails, tools, anything he'd simply needed to get out of the way. But his first night out, anchored off the Port Townsend beach rather than going ashore, he'd properly stowed everything that had been jammed in here.

Now, other than a few pillows having been knocked about by the storm, the cabin was pristine. The drawers were empty except for a few odds and ends: pens, paper, a clip-on light for reading a book at night—the light was still bright when he checked the battery. The bookshelf held a dictionary and thesaurus, new copies of the same ones he'd seen over Teresa's desk in Seattle. The narrow closet held...

He dropped onto the bed and instantly knew why he'd avoided this cabin. And why he'd left it empty even though space was at such a premium.

A brand-new set of deep-sea foul weather gear hung in the closet. He'd bought them when he'd purchased his own—the same day he'd bought the sailboat. He didn't need to check the label to remember that it was a women's medium. Teresa's size.

He'd made a space for her on his boat.

And she'd love it. He knew her well enough to be sure of that.

He'd been able to see her here. Sitting in a tropical

port, a light breeze drifting through the open portholes, working on her next book.

Ron had made a space for her on his boat.

But he hadn't made space for her in his life.

6

___

70 kilometers SSE of Honolulu

IT WAS RINGING.

Ron's radio could have been patched into a phone system to place this call at any time. But he'd delayed it until he could link to a Hawaiian cell tower. He didn't want to spread his shame all over the open airways, at least that's what he told himself.

Instead he'd stewed through five more days of sailing, sleeping almost as little as he had during the storm. The last eight hours, from when the towering summit of Mauna Kea had broken the horizon—his first sight of anything other than ocean in twenty-three days—until his phone had declared a single bar of signal, had been pure torture.

Then he'd delayed for another hour and five kilometers trying to figure out what to say. As if he hadn't done exactly that for the last five nights.

Second ring.

Third.

Oh crap! She wasn't going to pick up. She'd know it was him and—

"Hi, this is Teresa."

"Hey, it's me." Ron winced; she'd already know that.

Her voice continued. "I'm probably deep in solving a murder and I can't tear myself away. Or I'm in editing hell and can't face anyone. Leave your name and the title of your favorite book." Her voicemail beeped.

Hell! And damnation! And the curse of the sunken continent of Mu besides!

"I...uh... I didn't want to do this on voicemail. I'm... crap!" But maybe he was going to anyway. "I never asked. I should have asked. You know. If you wanted to come with me. Honestly I don't know what's wrong with me, so I'm hoping that you do. I'm coming up on Maui. Um, I'm fine. I hit a terrible storm, but *Brise* was a total champ. Exactly like you said, she made it a breeze. Okay, that was a white lie but none of it was her fault. And uh..." What? *Think, Ron. Think.* "My favorite book is you. Okay. Stupid and corny. Too corny for one of your books. But it's true. I miss you so much. No. That's not right. I mean yes I do. I really do. But it's more than that. What I mean to say—"

The beep cut him off.

"Shit!"

7

Lahaina Harbor
Maui, Hawaii

HE KEPT HIS PHONE CLOSE AND HE KEPT IT CHARGED—IT didn't ring.

Twenty-four hours. That's how long it took him from deciding that he couldn't call her back without getting all stalkery, to reaching the back side of Maui.

There'd been no sleep—again.

Sailing solo ain't so attractive now, is it, buddy boy?

Close around the Hawaiian Islands there were far too many boats to trust the autopilot. There also wasn't a lot of sea room here—it would be far too easy to run into an island while he slept. Instead of standing out to sea and turning about, he brewed coffee and kept watch.

The Vic-Maui International Yacht Race always landed in Lahaina Harbor. Twenty-five days ago he'd passed Victoria Harbor as he headed out the Strait of Juan de Fuca. The race winners would cover the same ground in half that time. Of course many of them would be in lean racing boats with full crews pushing the boat ahead every hour of the day and night.

He'd had offers to crew the Vic-Maui or the much longer return trip. What was two weeks downwind was a five- to six-week return, usually done by a pick-up crew. The skipper/owner would fly back to the Northwest, returning to their cushy day job, while the crew beat north until they could pick up the high Japanese Current and sweep down the Canadian coast.

But he'd never been able to justify the time off. All the years he'd lived on the West Coast and he'd never made it to Hawaiian Islands at all. Well now he had.

Welcome to Maui.

The water was the color he'd seen in a thousand photos but it was also something else entirely. The interplay of blues and turquoise was vibrantly alive in a way no photo could capture.

The birds. After weeks at sea without a single sighting, the birds were a shock, he hadn't missed that they were gone until they were back. A shearwater dove for fish. A white egret lofted by as casually as someone's grandparent. Ducks with brilliant red sides that he didn't recognize were busy along the shore. Small fish left circular rings on the smooth waters as they nipped bugs from the surface. The air and the water were vibrant with life.

It was evening as he sailed in close to Lahaina, lowered sails, and started the motor for the first time in three weeks.

As he nosed toward the small harbor behind the big

rock breakwater, the sun was sliding behind Lanai, the next island to the west. Already the turquoise was shifting to pick up the golds in the sky.

A coffee-klatch of pintail ducks scowled at him as they paddled aside when he passed too close.

He'd already prepped this lines and hung the fenders off the side, but there was still a lot to do all at once as he nosed carefully between the channel markers. According to the chart it had been dredged to two fathoms, twelve feet. But the harbor itself was only eight and he drew six-and-a-half. He should be safe at any tide, but he had no idea if he had inches or feet of leeway.

Check the tides first. Lesson for next time.

Past the channel markers, it quickly shoaled to three feet. *Brise* would not be happy if he drifted there.

Small sailboats flocked by, unconcerned by the shallows. A parasailing boat came off the beach, and raced off for a final evening run.

Made it! But he didn't like the question that followed immediately after, *Why?*

Lahaina Harbor, Lahaina, Maui, Hawaii.

It was the sort of place couples came for romantic getaways. Not the touristy types who massed at the big hotels and the thousand tacky boutiques designed to gather as much mainland money as possible and keep it in the islands. No, here the pace would be slower.

He and Teresa had talked about coming here. Okay, *he* had talked about it. He'd ride down the Vic-Maui, or come here to pick up a boat for the return. He hadn't considered stopping anywhere else in Hawaii as he'd now circled clear of the Big Island and bypassed the rest of

Maui to land at its westernmost point. This had simply been where he would come.

It did have the advantage of placing the mainland on the far side of the islands. He'd have to backtrack, pass the islands once more to head east toward home. So, from here he could launch *west* with that extra little barrier pushing him ahead toward the rest of the world.

Where?

Japan? Fiji? Guam? The Solomons?

It didn't matter. He'd stop here, top off his water tanks, and get fresh produce. He hadn't used any fuel, except to motor into the harbor here. Past that?

He wouldn't think about it.

The inner harbor was crazy. He was used to long sets of finger piers reaching out to either side of a primary dock.

Not here.

Lahaina Harbor was too small for that. It was a boulder-walled rectangle with mooring down both sides. Boats were rafted up side-to-side. Power boats were all parked stern in. The sailboats were all bow in. It would be dicey to pull it off single-handed. Not only did he have to come to a perfect stop with the bow at the edge of the perimeter walkway, but he'd also have to pick up one of the buoys floating out in the middle of the harbor to tie off his stern. All while manipulating the controls from the central cockpit.

Maybe he'd leave and anchor off the beach. Later he could come ashore in his dinghy if he had the energy. Or maybe tomorrow. It didn't matter.

He managed to make a three-point turn between the

two lines of boats without snagging any of the mid-channel buoys. His was definitely on the large side for this harbor. There were a couple of sixty-foot power yachts and several tourist boats with massive "Whale Watch" signs painted down the sides. But the common class here, in both sail and power, was down in the thirty-foot range.

Give it up! Anchor off the beach. Deal with life tomorrow.

Ron was easing back out of the harbor. Full dark was settling and he was cursing himself for not having anchored out in the *roads,* as the offshore stretches were called, to begin with.

A shout. He eased off the throttle and looked around.

"Aloha the sailboat!" He finally spotted the man standing at the end of the service pier and waved to show that he heard.

The man began gesturing him over.

He didn't need to fuel up now, but the gestures were insistent.

Ron had drifted past the dock, but easing into reverse, he crossed the rudder and slowly backed until he was turned and alongside the slip.

"No one else coming in here tonight," the man said as he leaned out to grab the line that Ron had preset along the gunwale. "Probably not tomorrow either. They can always use the other side of the pier."

With relief, Ron eased to a stop and hopped down to help tie off the boat.

He almost pitched off the other side of the pier because it didn't rock, unlike the boat.

The man laughed. "How long at sea?"

"Seattle." Ron braced his feet apart, but the pier didn't stop swaying though it was anchored to the sea bed. It was making him dizzy.

"Give it a day. Go for a swim. That'll set you up good."

Ron had heard about sea legs, but never been aboard a boat long enough to develop them before. He staggered up and down the dock securing *Brise* like a drunk in a hurricane. On land was the first time he'd felt queasy with seasickness in the whole trip.

Crawling back aboard, he made it as far as the cockpit. Stretching out on one of the benches, he stared up at the stars that had come out without his noticing. They'd all shifted strangely. Cygnus and Lyra, instead of being directly overhead were far to the north. As the sky continued to darken, the Milky Way put in an appearance far higher in the sky than he was used to.

His body begged for sleep.

But all his brain could do was think about Teresa not returning his call.

8

Lahaina Harbor
Maui, Hawaii

Ron bolted upright in the cockpit.

"I need a crew!"

He hadn't slept, but the moment of the dawn had brought absolute clarity.

He staggered down the dock, his balance about halfway back to normal for being off the sea, yet much worse for massive sleep derivation. That's why he needed a crew. The lack of sleep on the solo passage hadn't been safe. During that storm, he'd been lucky to not hallucinate a Seattle sidewalk and step of his boat into the ocean. He'd need a crew so that he could make the return run to Seattle fast.

By the time the service dock attendant who'd helped him last night showed up, he'd already filled half of the harbor's small Dumpster. He'd also found the *Free Stuff* shelf in the harbor office, which was unlocked, and buried it in his castoffs. There was always somewhere for boaters to exchange books or pass on old gear when new gear was acquired. He'd wager the bulk of his would be cleared out before the end of the day.

The few others who came off the boats to get breakfast in town offered him an *Aloha* and a wide berth.

Okay. Rationality running low. Definitely needed to refill that...somehow.

"I need a crew," he croaked out as soon as the attendant strolled up. He was a big guy with an easy smile, a brown-and-white Hawaiian shirt, and a trim beard gone half gray.

"Ease down, *brah*. Ease down. You've only just arrived." The man settled into a plastic chair in front of the office, a massive to-go coffee cup in his hand with the drawing of a mule on it. Below the drawing it said, *Bad Ass Coffee*. So, he held a massive to-go cup with the drawing of an *ass* on it.

Ron blinked to refocus. It didn't work until he'd done it a few times. He couldn't remember the man's name. He took a deep breath, but didn't feel any calmer.

"I need a crew, Akamu." Apparently a part of him had caught the guy's name last night.

"But—"

"A racing crew. Need the speed. Three at least." Ron sounded a little hysterical, even to himself. "Today would be really good."

"Where are you headed in such a hurry?"

"Seattle."

Akamu looked at him strangely. Then he glanced over at the stern of *Brise* as if checking his memory. Below the boat's name was the port of registry, Seattle, Washington, USA.

"You gone *lolo, brah?*"

Ron didn't need Akamu's expression to know he sounded like a crazy man.

"I—" It was stupid but, hey, since when was that news. "There's a girl. A woman. I left her behind. In Seattle." He held up his phone as if it meant something. Oh, it did. "She won't answer."

"*Shoots!*" Akamu acknowledged with a nod. He drank from his coffee cup as if there wasn't a reason in the world to hurry.

"I need—"

Akamu held up a hand to stop him.

Ron bit his tongue.

"Vic-Maui is next month, *brah*. The boat-bum return crews are starting to filter in, but they have come early to enjoy Hawaii."

In the sailing community, boat bum wasn't the insult it sounded. There were plenty of people who *bummed* a ride on various boats as a way of life for a summer or a year. They traded their crew skills for food and a free, if not fast, lift. If they were lucky, maybe enough spending money when they were done to hold them over until they found the next boat.

The Vic-Maui race was one of the hot rides because the owners desperately needed crew for the long haul of sailing their boats back to the Pacific Northwest. It was one of the longest races in the world that wasn't simply traveling a circle so that the boat and crew ended up where they'd started. It was over twice the length of the

Newport Bermuda Race, the other big ride for a boat bum.

Meaning he'd never find a crew unless he paid. Money he didn't really have. He'd sold his house for a lot more money than his boat, but that was supposed to support him for the long ride around the world. Which was years.

He dropped into a chair beside Akamu and stared at *Brise*. A typical circumnavigation by sail, without pushing, taking time to see places he was passing through, took three or four years.

That number hadn't really sunk in.

Had Teresa understood the scale of what he was doing? Probably. She was much better at that sort of thing than he was. She saw the consequences before he even understood the action.

Like a grown up. Silently telling himself to shut up? *Nope, didn't help.*

Maybe he should go home to Seattle. Give up the trip. Try to patch things up, if she'd let him.

"You could fly."

But if he did, would he ever come back? His dream floated fifty feet away. If he returned to Seattle? He could feel himself calling a boat broker in a few months to ship home his belongings and get what he could for the boat.

He now knew that the stories were true. Supposedly the cheapest places to buy a cruising boat were in the tropical paradises: Hawaii, Fiji, and Tahiti. Sailors set out and, unable to sustain their dreams, ultimately abandoned their boats.

Even after a few weeks' break, if he crawled back into the corporate grinder, some part of him would die.

Nope! Not the right answer.

"Where do I post signs?" he asked Akamu. Because the dream of sailing solo around the world was a naive one. He *could* do it, but what would be the point? He'd have stories that no one other than another deep-sea sailor would want to hear. And then what?

"Well," Akamu offered reluctantly, "there's a notice board at the head of the dock here. You might try down at the yacht club. You a member of another club, Seattle or something? They have these reciprocity agreements with a lot of places, if you're a member of one club, the other will let you in. Maybe use their e-mail list."

Ron laughed in Akamu's face and then had to explain. "The Seattle Yacht Club has a twenty-grand initiation fee, plus annual dues. You need multiple references from other members and it can take a year to be approved. I belong to the Sloop Tavern Yacht Club."

"Maybe they—"

"Their total annual fee is ninety dollars a year, fifty-five if you don't have a boat. It's traditional to buy a round for the bar when you pay your fee, which costs far more."

"Now *that* sounds like a proper yacht club!" Akamu joined in his laugh.

It felt good. Even with the lack of sleep and his flurry of activity this morning cleaning out the boat, that brief shared laugh felt good. What would it be like to sit here for a day? Or a week? Lay on a beach with a book for a day. There must be amazing wildlife and nature to see here. Hell, there's volcanos.

Maybe the dream wasn't dead. But alone? That wasn't right either.

He slouched in the chair and closed his eyes as Akamu chatted with some other boater in no hurry at all. Ron felt the warm sun at his back as it climbed over the shoulder of those big volcanos that had built the island. He'd never seen an active volcano before. Mt. St. Helens had exploded before he was born though the locals still talked about it like it was yesterday. It would be nice to see that. Maybe even tour the observatory atop one of the peaks. Sail around the other islands and see what else there was to see.

The other boater wandered away.

"Yes, *braddah,* sometimes you must simply sit and wait," Akamu said thoughtfully.

Ron didn't bother looking at him, or even opening his eyes. He could hear people returning from breakfast. There was slow-building flutter of noise. He half-blinked his eyes and saw them gathering under an *Atlantis Submarine Tour* sign.

The dock was alive, but it was all background. Muted. The long nights had caught up and he was almost asleep in his chair before Akamu spoke again.

"Maybe the goddess Laka is watching over you and *this* pretty lady wants to sail on your boat."

"Maybe," a voice from a dream.

He knew that voice. "Teresa," maybe he'd stay in this happy dream for awhile.

"Yes?"

He jolted upright and looked at her. He tried to shout, but was afraid that she was an apparition of Akamu's goddess. He began to reach out but feared she might be no more than a sleep-deprivation induced hallucination.

Teresa stood slightly hipshot, propping up a large backpack that rested beside her. Electric red sneakers with no socks and long legs to black denim shorts. She wore a red t-shirt he'd bought for her, showing an old typewriter and a scrolled out piece of paper stating, *I'm plotting a murder.* Her mop of unruly hair a dark blonde cap of curls. Honey-colored eyes and her smile...

"You're here." It was little more than a gasp.

Her smile grew.

"You're *really* here. You came."

Akamu chuckled but didn't interrupt.

"To sail?"

She shrugged and he didn't know what to say to that.

He looked at Akamu who rolled his eyes at him. Ron still didn't get it.

Finally Teresa took pity on him, as he recalled she often had to do.

She took a step closer, letting her pack flop down onto the dock and set her computer bag on top of it—both were stuffed to the gills.

"You have to remember to *ask.*"

He'd never actually asked if she would sail with him.

Too afraid that the answer would be no? Or because he was a complete idiot?

Didn't matter.

She was here.

Here with that big pack and her laptop bag. She'd always said she could write anywhere as long as she had her computer and a supply of caffeine-free diet Coke. He had plenty of the latter on board though he rarely drank it himself.

Ron struggled to his feet. When he brushed at her cheek, she leaned into it. When he kissed her, she kissed him back so gently that it was far more promise than anything physical.

"I need to ask. Right. I'll," he had to clear his throat again to speak. "I'll keep that in mind for the future."

This time the kiss was a promise for a long future ahead.

———

If you enjoyed this story
please consider leaving a review.
They really help.

Keep reading for an exciting excerpt from:
Where Dreams #1: *Where Dreams are Born*

WHERE DREAMS ARE BORN (EXCERPT)

IF YOU ENJOYED THAT, YOU'LL LOVE THIS TALE!

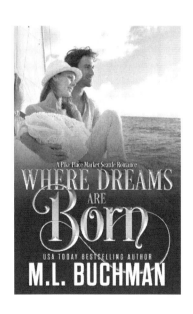

WHERE DREAMS ARE BORN
(EXCERPT)

RUSSELL LEANED HIS BACK AGAINST THE STUDIO DOOR after he locked it behind the last of the staff. He barely managed the energy to turn off his camera.

He knew it was good. The images were there; he'd really captured them.

But something was missing.

The groove ran so clean when he slid into it. First his Manhattan high-ceilinged loft would fade into the background, then the strobe lights, reflector umbrellas, and green-screen backdrops all became texture and tone.

Image, camera, and man then became one and nothing else mattered—a single flow of light, beginning before time was counted, and ending its journey in the printed image. One ray of primordial light traveling forever to glisten off the BMW roadster still parked in one corner of the rough-planked wood floor worn smooth by generations of use. Another ray lost in the dark blackness of the finest leather bucket seats. A hundred more picking out the supermodel's perfect hand dangling a single shining and golden key—the image shot just slow enough that the key blurred as it spun, but the logo remained clear.

He couldn't quite put his finger on it...

It would be another great ad by Russell Morgan, Inc. The client would be knocked dead—the ad leaving all others standing still as it roared down the passing lane. This one might get him another Clio, or even a second Mobius.

But...

There wasn't usually a "but."

And there definitely wasn't supposed to be one.

The groove had definitely been there, but he hadn't been in it.

That was the problem. It had slid along, sweeping his staff into their own orchestrated perfection, but he'd remained untouched. That ideal, seamless flow hadn't included him at all.

"Be honest, boyo, that session sucked," he told the empty studio. Everything had come together so perfectly for yet another ad for yet another high-end glossy. *Man, the Magazine* would launch spectacularly in a few weeks, a high-profile mid-December launch, and it would include a never before seen twelve-page spread by the great Russell Morgan. The rag would probably never pay off the lavish launch party of hope, ice sculptures, and chilled magnums of champagne before disappearing like a thousand before it.

"Morose much?"

The studio kept its thoughts to itself—the first reliable sign that he wasn't totally losing his shit.

He stowed the last camera with the others piled by his computer. At the breaker box he shut off the umbrellas, spots, scoops, and washes. The studio shifted from a stark landscape in hard-edged relief to a nest of curious shadows and rounded forms. The tang of hot metal and deodorant were the only lasting result of the day's efforts.

"Get your shit together, Russell." His reflection in the darkened window, stories above the streetlights of West 10th, was unimpressed and proved it was wise enough to not answer back. There was never a "down" after a shoot; there was always an "up."

Not tonight.

He'd kept everyone late—even though it was Thanksgiving eve—hoping for that smooth slide of image-camera-man. It was only when he saw the power of the images he captured that he knew he wasn't a part of the chain anymore and decided he'd paid enough triple-time expenses.

The next to last two-page spread would be the killer —shot with the door open against a background as black as the sports car's finish, the model's single perfect leg wrapped in thigh-high red-leather boots all that was visible in the driver's seat. The sensual juxtaposition of woman and sleek machine served as an irresistible focus. It was an ad designed to wrap every person with even a hint of a Y-chromosome around its little finger. And those with only X-chromosomes would simply want to be her. He'd shot a perfect combo of sex for the guys and power for the women.

Even the final one-page image, a close-up of driver's seat from exactly the same angle, revealing not the model but instead a single rose of precisely the same hue as the leather boot, hadn't moved him despite its perfection.

Without him noticing, Russell had become no more than the observer, merely a technician behind the camera. Now that he faced it, months, maybe even a year had passed since he'd been yanked all the way into the light-image-camera-man slipstream. Tonight was a wakeup call and he didn't like it one bit. Wakeup calls happened to others, not him. But tonight he could no longer ignore it, he hadn't even trailed along in the churned-up wake.

"You're just a creative cog in the advertising machine." Ouch! That one stung, but it didn't turn aside the relentless steamroller of his thoughts speeding down some empty, godforsaken autobahn.

His career was roaring ahead, his business' growth running fast and smooth. But, now that he considered it, he really didn't give a damn.

His life looked perfect, but—"Don't think it!"—his autobahn mind finished despite the command, *it wasn't.*

Russell left his silent reflection to its own thoughts and went through the back door that led to his apartment —closing it tightly on the perfect BMW, the perfect rose, and somewhere, lost among a hundred other props from dozens of other shoots, the long pair of perfect red-leather Chanel boots that had been wrapped around the most expensive legs in Manhattan. He didn't care if he never walked back through that door again. He'd been doing his art by rote; how god-awful sad was that?

And just to rub salt in the wound, he shot *commercial* art.

He'd never had the patience to do art for art's sake. Delayed gratification was his idea of no fun at all. He left the apartment dark with only the city's soft glow through the blind-covered windows revealing the vaguest outlines of the framed art on the wall. Even that almost overwhelmed him tonight.

He didn't want to see the huge prints by the *art* artists: autographed Goldsworthy, Liebowitz, and Joseph Francis' photomosaics for the moderns. A hundred and fifty rare, even one-of-a-kind prints adorned his walls—all the way back through Bourke-White to Russell's prize, an original Daguerre. The Museum of Modern Art kept begging to borrow his collection for a show...and at the moment he was half tempted to dump the whole lot in their Dumpster if they didn't want it.

Crossing the one-room loft apartment—as spacious as the studio—he bypassed the circle of avant-garde chairs that were almost as uncomfortable as they looked and avoided the lush black-leather wrap-around sectional sofa of such ludicrous scale that it could be a playpen for two or host a party for twenty. He cracked the fridge in the stainless-steel-and-black corner kitchen searching for something other than his usual beer.

A bottle of Krug.

Maybe he was just being grouchy after a long day's work.

Juice.

No. He'd run his enthusiasm into the ground but good.

Milk even.

Would he miss the camera if he never picked it up again?

No reaction.

Nothing.

Not even an itch in his palm.

That was an emptiness he did not want to face. Especially not alone, in his apartment, in the middle of the world's most vibrant city.

Russell turned away, and just as the door swung closed, the last sliver of light—the relentless chilly blue-white of the refrigerator bulb—shone across his bed. A quick grab snagged the edge of the door and left the narrow beam illuminating a long pale form on his black-silk bedspread.

The Chanel boots weren't in the studio after all. They were still wrapped around those three thousand dollar-an-hour legs: the only clothing on a perfect body. Five foot-eleven of intensely toned female anatomy right down to an exquisitely stair-mastered behind. Her long, white-blonde hair lay as a perfect Godiva over her tanned breasts—except for their too exact symmetry, even the closest inspection didn't reveal the work done there. She lay with one leg raised just ever so slightly to hide what was meant to be revealed later.

Melanie.

By the steady rise and fall of her flat stomach, he knew she'd fallen asleep while waiting for him to finish in the studio.

How long had they been an item? Two months? Three?

She'd made him feel alive...at least when he was

actually with her. Melanie was the super-model in his bed or on his arm at yet another SoHo gallery opening. Together they journeyed to sharp parties and trendy three-star restaurants where she dazzled and wooed yet another gathering of New York's finest with her ever so soft, so sensual, and so studied French accent. Together they were wired into the heart of the in-crowd.

But that wasn't him, was it? It didn't sound like the Russell he once knew.

Perhaps "they" were about how *he* looked on *her* arm?

Did she know tomorrow was the annual Thanksgiving ordeal at his parents? The grand holiday gathering that he'd rather die than attend? Any number of eligible woman would be floating about his parents' house out in Greenwich; anyone able to finagle an invitation would attend in hopes of snaring one of *People Magazine's* "100 Most Eligible." They all wanted to land the heir to a billion or some such; though he was wealthy enough on his own, by his own sweat, to draw anyone's attention. He ranked number twenty-four on the list this year—up from forty-seven the year before despite Tom Cruise being available yet again.

But not Melanie. He knew that it wasn't the money that drew her. Yes, she wanted him. But even more, she wanted the life that came with him—wrapped in the man-package. She wanted The Life. The one that *People Magazine* readers dreamed about between glossy pages.

His fingertips were growing cold where they held the refrigerator door cracked open.

If he woke her there'd be amazing sex. Or a great party to go to. Or...

Did he want "Or"? What more did he want from her?

Sex. Companionship. An energy, a vivacity, a thirst he feared that he lacked. Yes.

But where was that smooth synchronicity hiding, like the light-image-camera-man of photography that he'd lost? Where lurked that perfect flow from one person to another? Did she feel it? Could he ever feel it? Did it even exist?

"More?" he whispered into the darkness to test the sound. He knew all about wanting more.

The refrigerator door slid shut—escaping from his numbed fingers—which plunged the apartment back into darkness, taking Melanie along with it.

His breath echoed in the vast darkness. Proof that he was alive if nothing more.

It was time to close the studio—time to be done with Russell Incorporated.

Then what?

Maybe Angelo would know what to do. He always claimed that he did. Maybe this time Russell would actually listen to his almost-brother, though he knew from the experience of being himself for the last thirty years that was unlikely.

Seattle.

Damn! He'd have to go to bloody Seattle to find his best friend. There was a possible upside to such a trip— maybe there'd be a flight out before tomorrow's mess at his parents'. He slapped his pocket, but once again he'd set his phone down in some unknown corner of the studio and it would take forever to find. He really needed two—one chained down so that he could always find it to call the other.

Russell considered the darkness. He could guarantee that Seattle wouldn't be a big hit with Melanie.

Now if he only knew whether that was a good thing or bad.

———

Keep reading now!
A great tale of romance and adventure,
Of sailboats, food, fashion, and fun.
Available at fine retailers everywhere.
Where Dreams are Born

And please don't forget that review for Solo Passage.

ABOUT THE AUTHOR

USA Today and Amazon #1 Bestseller M. L. "Matt" Buchman has 70+ action-adventure thriller and military romance novels, 100 short stories, and lotsa audiobooks. PW says: "Tom Clancy fans open to a strong female lead will clamor for more." Booklist declared: "3X Top 10 of the Year." A project manager with a geophysics degree, he's designed and built houses, flown and jumped out of planes, solo-sailed a 50' sailboat, and bicycled solo around the world...and he quilts. More at: www. mlbuchman.com.

Other works by M. L. Buchman: (* - also in audio)

Action-Adventure Thrillers

Dead Chef
One Chef!
Two Chef!

Miranda Chase
Drone*
Thunderbolt*
Condor*
Ghostrider*
Raider*
Chinook*
Havoc*
White Top*
Start the Chase*

Science Fiction / Fantasy

Deities Anonymous
Cookbook from Hell: Reheated
Saviors 101

Single Titles
Monk's Maze
the Me and Elsie Chronicles

Contemporary Romance

Eagle Cove
Return to Eagle Cove
Recipe for Eagle Cove
Longing for Eagle Cove
Keepsake for Eagle Cove

Love Abroad
Heart of the Cotswolds: England
Path of Love: Cinque Terre, Italy

Where Dreams
Where Dreams are Born
Where Dreams Reside
Where Dreams Are of Christmas*
Where Dreams Unfold
Where Dreams Are Written
Where Dreams Continue

Non-Fiction

Strategies for Success
Managing Your Inner Artist/Writer
Estate Planning for Authors*
Character Voice
Narrate and Record Your Own
Audiobook*

Short Story Series by M. L. Buchman:

Action-Adventure Thrillers

Dead Chef

Miranda Chase Origin Stories

Romantic Suspense

Antarctic Ice Fliers

US Coast Guard

Contemporary Romance

Eagle Cove

Other

Deities Anonymous (fantasy)

Single Titles

The Emily Beale Universe
(military romantic suspense)

The Night Stalkers
MAIN FLIGHT
The Night Is Mine
I Own the Dawn
Wait Until Dark
Take Over at Midnight
Light Up the Night
Bring On the Dusk
By Break of Day
Target of the Heart
Target Lock on Love
Target of Mine
Target of One's Own
NIGHT STALKERS HOLIDAYS
*Daniel's Christmas**
*Frank's Independence Day**
*Peter's Christmas**
Christmas at Steel Beach
*Zachary's Christmas**
*Roy's Independence Day**
*Damien's Christmas**
Christmas at Peleliu Cove

Henderson's Ranch
*Nathan's Big Sky**
*Big Sky, Loyal Heart**
*Big Sky Dog Whisperer**
*Tales of Henderson's Ranch**

Shadow Force: Psi
*At the Slightest Sound**
*At the Quietest Word**
*At the Merest Glance**
*At the Clearest Sensation**

White House Protection Force
*Off the Leash**
*On Your Mark**
*In the Weeds**

Firehawks
Pure Heat
Full Blaze
*Hot Point**
*Flash of Fire**
Wild Fire
SMOKEJUMPERS
*Wildfire at Dawn**
*Wildfire at Larch Creek**
*Wildfire on the Skagit**

Delta Force
*Target Engaged**
*Heart Strike**
*Wild Justice**
*Midnight Trust**

Emily Beale Universe Short Story Series

The Night Stalkers
The Night Stalkers Stories
The Night Stalkers CSAR
The Night Stalkers Wedding Stories
The Future Night Stalkers

Delta Force
Th Delta Force Shooters
The Delta Force Warriors

Firehawks
The Firehawks Lookouts
The Firehawks Hotshots
The Firebirds

White House Protection Force
Stories

Future Night Stalkers
Stories (Science Fiction)

SIGN UP FOR M. L. BUCHMAN'S NEWSLETTER TODAY

and receive:
Release News
Free Short Stories
a Free Book

Get your free book today. Do it now.
free-book.mlbuchman.com

Printed in Great Britain
by Amazon